Society of American Artists

Society Of American Artists

Fourth Annual Exhibition 1881

Society of American Artists

Society Of American Artists
Fourth Annual Exhibition 1881

ISBN/EAN: 9783337299804

Printed in Europe, USA, Canada, Australia, Japan

Cover: Foto ©Andreas Hilbeck / pixelio.de

More available books at **www.hansebooks.com**

SOCIETY

OF

AMERICAN ARTISTS

FOURTH ANNUAL

EXHIBITION

OPEN FROM MARCH 28TH
UNTIL APRIL 29TH

FROM 9 A. M. TO 6 P. M. AND FROM 7.30 P. M. TO 10 P. M.

On Sundays from 2 P. M. to 5 P. M.   Free by tickets to be obtained on application
at Brentano's, 39 Union Square, and Putnam's, 182 5th Avenue.

NEW YORK
1881

SOCIETY

OF

AMERICAN ARTISTS

AUGUSTUS ST. GAUDENS, President
J. ALDEN WEIR, Vice-President
FREDERICK DIELMAN, Secretary
FRANCIS LATHROP, Treasurer

WALTER SHIRLAW
HELENA DE KAY
R. SWAIN GIFFORD
HOMER D. MARTIN
JOHN LA FARGE
WILL H. LOW
A. H. WYANT
J. H. DOLPH
CHAS. H. MILLER
D. MAITLAND ARMSTRONG
JOHN H. TWACHTMAN
ABBOT H. THAYER
S. W. VAN SCHAICK
F. C. P. VINTON
J. M. STONE
GEO. W. MAYNARD
FRANK D. MILLET
THEODORE BAUR
J. C. BECKWITH
J. FRANK CURRIER

WYATT EATON
OLIN L. WARNER
LOUIS C. TIFFANY
SAMUEL COLMAN
WILLIAM SARTAIN
ROBERT C. MINOR
GEORGE INNESS
ALBERT P. RYDER
WM. M. CHASE
W. R. O'DONOVAN
WM. GEDNEY BUNCE
JOHN S. SARGENT
T. W. DEWING
J. FOXCROFT COLE
SARAH W. WHITMAN
DOUGLAS VOLK
MARY CASSATT
GEO. INNESS, Jr.
GEO. D. BRUSH
FRANK DUVENECK

CHARLES MELVILLE DEWEY.

CATALOGUE.

Information in regard to Works for Sale, &c., may be had at the desk in the Gallery.

All payments should be made before the close of the Exhibition to the order of **FRANCIS LATHROP**, Treasurer.

NO.	SUBJECT.	OWNER OR PRICE.	ARTIST.
1	*Spring,*	*The Artist,*	*Geo. Inness.*
2	*Twilight,*	*$200.00*	*J. Francis Murphy.*
3	*Among the Reeds,*	*Dr. Wynkoop.*	*Douglas Volk.*
4	*Study of a Man Sneezing,*	*100.00*	*Edw. Dowdall.*
5	*Portrait of a Baby,*	*Arthur Parton,*	*J. Carroll Beckwith.*
6	*The Prayer,*	*200.00*	*S. W. Van Schaick.*
7	*Street by the Ramparts,*	*For Sale, .*	*William Sartain.*
8	*A Frugal Meal,*	*.*	*Alfred Kappes.*
9	*Twins,*	*150.00*	*Th. Robinson.*
10	*Daffodils,*	*.*	*E. B. Greene.*
11	*Sketch,*	*75.00*	*Fred. W. Freer.*
12	*Landscape,*	*For Sale,*	*A. M. Farnham.*
13	*Boy in Red,*	*Geo. C. Cooper,*	*J. Frank Currier.*
14	*Study,*	*.*	*Thomas Hovenden.*
15	*The Letter,*	*For Sale, .*	*Walter McEwen.*

NO.	SUBJECT.	OWNER OR PRICE.	ARTIST.
16	Portrait of Miss L.J.	J. F. J., Esq.,	Wyatt Eaton.
17	Head,	.	John Selinger.
18	The Hay Cart,	.	H. Bisbing.
19	Landscape,	For Sale, .	J. H. Twachtman.
20	Portrait,	The Artist,	Abbott H. Thayer.
21	Lady Singing a Pathetic Song,	1,200.00	Thos. Eakins.
22	Portrait,	. .	Abbott H. Thayer.
23	Landscape,	For Sale,	J. Frank Currier.
24	A Lesson in Housekeeping,	150.00	Frank C. Jones.
25	In Venice,	250.00	Wm. M. Chase.
26	Joan of Arc,	.	J. Bastien-Lepage.
27	The Giudecca, Venice,	For Sale, .	William Sartain.
28	Kathleen,	The Artist,	Geraldine Reed.
29	Portrait,	.	Abbott H. Thayer.
30	French Court-yard,	175.00	Frank Fowler.
30a	A Breezy Day in June,	800.00	J. Appleton Brown.
31	Spanish Gypsy,	200.00	Wm. T. Dannat.
32	Twilight,	175.00	Frank Fowler.
33	Morning,	.	Homer Martin.
34	Editor's Sanctum,	250.00	Lyell Carr.
35	The End of a Storm,	The Artist,	Geo. Inness.
36	After the Rain,	.	Arthur Quartley.

NO.	SUBJECT.	OWNER OR PRICE.	ARTIST.
37	*Skipper Ireson,*	$2.000.00 .	*Will H. Low.*

Then the wife of the skipper lost at sea
Said, "God has touched him! why should we?"
Said an old wife, mourning her only son,
"Cut the rogue's tether and let him run!"
So, with soft relentings and rude excuse,
Half scorn, half pity, they cut him loose,
And gave him a cloak to hide him in,
And left him alone with his shame and sin.
Poor Floyd Ireson, for his hard heart
Tarred and feathered and carried in a cart
By the women of Marblehead.
Skipper Ireson's Ride.—JOHN GREENLEAF WHITTIER.

38	*In the Valley,*	475.00	*Hamilton Hamilton.*
39	*Moonlight,*	*For Sale,*	*W. P. W. Dana.*
40	*October near South Orange, N. J.,*	*The Artist,*	*H. Bolton Jones.*
41	*Portrait,*	.	*Abbott H. Thayer.*
42	*Landscape,*	300.00	*Walter L. Palmer.*
43	*The Advance,*	200.00	*J. M. Stone.*
44	*Bull-fighter,*	. .	*E. H. Blashfield.*
45	*Landscape and Cattle*	*T. Cole,* .	*Abbott H. Thayer.*
46	*Landscape,*	500.00 .	*Wm. M. Chase.*
47	*Interior of Studio,*	*Mr.Saml.M.Dodd,*	*Wm. M. Chase.*
48	*Portrait of Miss A. F.,*	*Hon. C. B. F.,*	*Wyatt Eaton.*
49	*A Reminiscence of Sicily,*		*Geo. Fuller.*
50	*An Old Tree at Non-quitt,*	*For Sale,*	*William Sartain.*
51	*Venezia,*	.	*Wm. Gedney Bunce.*

NO.	SUBJECT.	OWNER OR PRICE.	ARTIST.
52		*Rev.N.W.Conkling, A. P. Ryder.*	

In splendor rare, the moon,
In full-orbed splendor,
On sea and darkness making light.
While windy spaces and night,
In all vastness, did make,
With cattled hill and lake,
A scene grand and lovely.
Then, gliding above the
Dark water, a lover's boat,
In quiet beauty, did float
Upon the scene, mingling shadows
Into the deeper shadows
Of sky and land reflected.

53	*Garden of the Old Monastery,*	400.00	*Wm. M. Chase.*
54	*Portrait,*	*The Artist,* .	*Geo. D. Brush.*
55	*Portrait,*	*Mr.Warren Delano*	*J. Alden Weir.*
56	*A New England Hillside,*	350.00	*W. S. Macy.*
57	*Portrait in Costume,*	.	*F. D. Millet.*
58	*The Great Bog, South of Tralee, Ireland.*	500.00	*A. H. Wyant.*
59	*Pink Roses,*	100.00 .	*E. B. Greene.*
60	*Holland Apples,*	*Cottier & Co.,* .	*Wm. Gedney Bunce.*
61	*Tenth Street Dock,*	*For Sale,* .	*J. H. Twachtman.*
62	*Andante,*	750.00	{ *Fred. W. Freer,* { *T. W. Dewing.*
63	*The Fugitive,*	*For Sale,*	*L. B. Harrison.*
64	*The Truant Abroad.*	. .	*Gilbert Gaul.*
65	*" Companions,"*	*For Sale,* .	*Frederick Dielman.*

NO.	SUBJECT.	OWNER OR PRICE.	ARTIST.
66	Evening,	$75.00	Geo. W. Maynard.
67	Impression of a Rainy Night, N.Y.,	For Sale, .	J. H. Lungren.
68	In the Fields,	200.00	Rosina Emmet.
69	Music and Dance—a Panel for Decoration,	Edw. A. Wickes.	Francis Lathrop.
70	The Beach Road,	300.00 .	R. Swain Gifford.
71	A Prelude,	Mr. Cyrus Butler,	Wm. M. Chase.
72	Wisconsin Pastoral,	75.00	Th. Robinson.
73	Capri Peasant—Study,		John S. Sargent.
74	Portrait of Miss M. G. R.,	Mrs. S. R.,	Wyatt Eaton.
75	Still Life—Fruit,	225.00	W. T. Dannat.
76	November—Mt. Desert, Maine,		Wm. Gedney Bunce.
77	Study,	. .	John La Farge.
78	Music,	1,500.00	J. Alden Weir.
79	A Concert,	For Sale, .	T. W. Dewing.
80	White Roses,	.	E. B. Greene.
81	Nebo,	300.00	Wm. Gedney Bunce.
82	Suburbs of Cincinnati	For Sale, .	J. H. Twachtman.
83	Flowers,	The Artist,	C. Wheeler.
84	Corner of a Studio,	350.00 .	Wm. T. Dannat.
85	Flowers,	Mrs. D. C. Eaton.	J. Alden Weir.
86	Study of a Peasant Girl,		John Selinger.
87	Pasture,		Fred. W. Freer.

NO.	SUBJECT.	OWNER OR PRICE.	ARTIST.
88	Portrait,	The Artist,	Abbott H. Thayer.
89	Horse's Head,	. .	G. W. Brenneman.
90	In the Orange Grove	450.00	George B. Butler, Jr.
91	Study of a Head,	For Sale, . .	William Sartain.
92	Portrait of Mr. B.,	Mrs. H. Hadden.	John S. Sargent.
93	A Mountain Path through Cedars,	250.00	R. A. Blakelock.
93a	Telegraph Station, Sandy Hook,	300.00	R. Swain Gifford.
94	August Among the Apple Trees,	For Sale, .	Charles M. Dewey.
95	A Sketch from Nature,	For Sale, .	D. M. Bunker.
96	Portrait of a Boy,		Abbott H. Thayer.
97	Portrait,		Rosina Emmet.
98	Sunset at Purgatory Newport, R. I.,	For Sale, .	Chas. H. Miller.
99	A Portrait,	. . .	Eastman Johnson.
100	A Portrait,	Rev. G. W. Dorrance	Geo. W. Maynard.
101	Connecticut Pasture,	Mrs. I. C. Eaton.	J. H. Niemeyer.
102	Marblehead Harbor,	300.00 .	J. Foxcroft Cole.
103	Landscape — Autumn,	E. P. Fabbri,	J. Alden Weir.
104	Ralph Waldo Emerson,		D. C. French.
105	Portrait Bust—Mr. Cabot,		D. C. French.
106	The Dancing Nymph		Olin L. Warner.
107	Portrait of Two Boys,	.	Augustus St. Gaudens.

NO.	SUBJECT.	OWNER OR PRICE.	ARTIST.
108	Kid's Head in Bronze,	$12.00	Paul W. Bartlett.
109	Rodman DeKay Gilder,		Augustus St. Gaudens.
110	Portrait,		Augustus St. Gaudens.
111	Medallion Portrait of Geo. Jones, Esq.,	Geo. Jones,	Olin L. Warner.
112	Portrait of Doctor Henry Shiff,	. . .	Augustus St. Gaudens.
113	J. Bastien-Lepage,	Scribner's Monthly,	Augustus St. Gaudens. Eng.by Fred Juengling
114	Study for Portrait of Doellinger, after Lenbach,	Scribner's Monthly,	Eng.by Fred Juengling
115	Portrait, Thomas Carlyle,	Scribner & Co.,	Eng. from Photo. by T. Cole.
116–133	Sketches in Venice—eighteen Etchings,		Otto H. Bacher.
134	Portrait of a Lady, after Wm.M.Chase,	Am. Art Review.	Eng.by Fred Juengling
135	J. Bastien-Lepage,		Augustus St. Gaudens.
136	Portrait Bust of Miss Maud Morgan,		Olin L. Warner.
137	Crayon Portrait of Mrs.W.W.L., Jr.,	W.W.L., Jr., Esq.,	Wyatt Eaton.
138	The Dance,	400.00 .	Robt. Blum.
139	Medallion Portrait of a Lady,		Olin L. Warner.

NO.	SUBJECT.	OWNER OR PRICE.	ARTIST.
140	*The Roadside Murder,*	125.00	*G. W. Brenneman.*
141	*Barn-yard,*		*John Ward Stimpson.*
142	*Very Old, after Walter Shirlaw,*	*Am. Art Review,*	*Eng. by Fred Juengling*
143	*Quiet Place,*	100.00	*R. Bruce Crane.*
144	*Clay Relief—Study of a Head,*		*Hoburt B. Jacobs.*
145	*Summer Flowers,*	.	*Wm. Prettyman.*
146	*Water Lilies,*	50.00	*Josephine B. Kibbe.*
147	*Winter Sunshine,*	*For Sale,*	*J. H. Niemeyer.*

EXHIBITORS.

Bacher, Otto H.—116—133.
Bartlett, Paul W., 394 Federal Street, Boston. Mass.—108.
Bastien-Lepage, Jules, Damvilliers, Meuse, France—26.
Beckwith, J. Carroll, 58 W. 57th Street—5.
Bisbing, H., Philadelphia, Pa.—18.
Blakelock, R. A., 355 W. 22d Street—93.
Blashfield, E. H., 849 Broadway—44.
Blum, Robt., 58 W. 57th Street—138.
Brenneman, G. W., 11 E. 14th Street—89, 140.
Brown, J. Appleton, 5 Park Street, Boston—30a.
Brush, Geo. D., San Francisco—54.
Bunce, Wm. Gedney, 80 E. Washington Square—51, 60, 76, 81.
Bunker, D. M., 788 Broadway—95.
Butler, George B., Jr.—90.

Carr, Lyell, 1267 Broadway—34.
Chase, Wm. M., 51 W. 10th Street—25, 46, 47, 53, 71.
Cole, J. Foxcroft, 433 Washington Street, Boston—102.
Cole, T.—115.
Crane, R. Bruce—143.
Currier, J. Frank, Munich, Bavaria—13, 23.

Dana, W. P. W.—39.
Dannat, W. T., The Knickerbocker, 14th Street and Fifth Ave.—
Dewey, Charles Melville, 788 Broadway—94.   [31, 75, 84.

Dewing, T.W., 68 *University Building, Washington Square*—62, 79.
Dielman, Frederick, 146 *E.* 40*th Street*—65.
Dowdall, Edw., 824 *Broadway*—4.

Eakins, Thos., 1729 *Mt. Vernon Street, Philadelphia*—21.
Eaton, Wyatt, 153 *Fourth Avenue*—16, 48, 74, 137.
Emmet, Rosina, 51 *W.* 10*th Street*- 68, 97.

Farnham, A. M.—12.
Fowler, Frank, University Building, Washington Square— 30, 32.
Freer, Fred. W., 61 *University Building, Washington Square*—11.
French, D. C., Concord, Mass.—104, 105.   [62, 87.
Fuller, Geo., Boston, Mass.—49.

Gaul, Gilbert, 51 *W.* 10*th Street*—64.
Gifford, R. Swain, 52 *E.* 23*d Street*—70, 93*a*.
Greene, E. B., 20 *Cedar Street, Boston, Mass.*—10, 59, 80.

Hamilton, Hamilton, Booth's Building, Sixth Ave. and 23*d Street*-38.
Harrison, L. B., 108 *Queen Street, Germantown, Pa.*—63.
Hovenden, Thomas, 58 *W.* 57*th Street*—14.

Inness, Geo., University Building, Washington Square—1, 35.

Jacobs, Hoburt B., 1267 *Broadway*—144.
Johnson, Eastman, 65 *W.* 55*th Street*—99.
Jones, H. Bolton, 58 *W.* 57*th Street*—40.
Jones, Frank C., 58 *W.* 57*th Street*—24.
Juengling, Fred., 220 *E.* 48*th Street*—113, 114, 134, 142.

Selinger, John, 42 *Wilcox Building, Providence, R. I.*—17, 86.
Stimpson, John Ward—141.
Stone, J. M., Boston, Mass.—43.   [20, 22, 29, 41, 45, 88, 96.

Thayer, Abbott H., Y. M.C.A. Building, 23d *St. and Fourth Ave.*—
Twachtman, J. H., Florence, Italy—19, 61, 82.

Van Schaick, S. W., Florence, Italy—6.
Volk, Douglas, 109 *W.* 34th *Street*—3.

Warner, Olin L., 80 *E. Washington Square*—106, 111, 136, 139.
Weir, J. Alden, 80 *E. Washington Square*—55, 78, 85, 103.
Wheeler, C., 335 *Fourth Avenue*—83.
Wyant, A. H., 58 *W.* 57th *Street*—58.

www.ingramcontent.com/pod-product-compliance
Lightning Source LLC
Chambersburg PA
CBHW020627260626
47157CB00009B/3205